Magic Mix-Up!

Look out for more stories...

Airy Fairy

Magic Mix-Up!

Margaret Ryan

illustrated by Teresa Murfin

BARRON'S

Spotlight

visit us at www.abdopublishing.com

Reinforced library bound edition published in 2010 by Spotlight, a division of the ABDO Group, 8000 West 78th Street, Edina, Minnesota 55439. This edition was reprinted with permission of Barron's Educational Series, Inc.

To Millie, with love

First edition for the United States, the Philippines, and Canada published by Barron's Educational Series, Inc., 2005. First published by Scholastic Ltd, 2005. All inquiries should be addressed to: Barron's Educational Series, Inc., 250 Wireless Boulevard, Hauppauge, New York 11788.
www.barronseduc.com

Text copyright © Margaret Ryan, 2005
Illustrations copyright © Teresa Murfin, 2005

Library of Congress Cataloging-in-Publication Data
Ryan, Margaret, 1944-
 Airy Fairy / Margaret Ryan ; illustrated by Teresa Murfin. -- Reinforced library bound ed.
   v. cm.
 Contents: bk. 1. Magic mess! -- bk. 2. Magic mischief! -- bk. 3. Magic mistakes! -- bk. 4. Magic mix-up! -- bk. 5. Magic muddle! -- bk. 6. Magic music!
 ISBN 978-1-59961-497-7 (bk. 1) -- ISBN 978-1-59961-498-4 (bk. 2) -- ISBN 978-1-59961-499-1 (bk. 3) -- ISBN 978-1-59961-500-4 (bk. 4) -- ISBN 978-1-59961-501-1 (bk. 5) -- ISBN 978-1-59961-502-8 (bk. 6)
 [1. Fairies--Fiction. 2. Orphans--Fiction. 3. Schools--Fiction.] I. Murfin, Teresa, ill. II. Title.

PZ7.R9543Ai 2009
[Fic]--dc22   2008033394

All Spotlight books have reinforced library binding
and are manufactured in the United States of America.

Chapter One

It was the last day of the summer term at Fairy Gropplethorpe's Academy for Good Fairies and the fairies were busy cleaning out their desks.

"Be sure to clear out all the trash," said their teacher, Miss Stickler, "and put it in the bin."

Airy Fairy stopped gazing out of the classroom window at the swallows flying by, lifted up the lid of her desk, and stuck her head inside. "My desk's not really full of trash," she said to her friends, Buttercup and Tingle. "It's just full of things that might be really useful one day. Like this empty yogurt container. I could keep all my pens and pencils in it." And she carefully placed them into it and sat it on top of her desk. Then she opened her desk lid again, knocked over the yogurt container, and scattered the pens and pencils onto the floor.

"Oops," she said, and bent to pick them up.

Scary Fairy, whose desk was always neat, smiled slyly and waved her little wand. Suddenly, the pens and pencils started rolling all over the floor. Airy Fairy crawled around after them, but as soon as she reached out for them, they rolled even further away.

"Airy Fairy, what ARE you doing?" frowned Miss Stickler, when she saw Airy Fairy's bottom sticking up in the air.

"Sorry, Miss Stickler," gasped Airy Fairy, standing up and banging her head on Scary Fairy's desk. "I was trying to pick up my pens and pencils. They keep rolling away from me."

"Nonsense," said Miss Stickler, looking at the now perfectly still pens and pencils. "Pick them up at once and get on with your cleaning."

"Yes, Miss Stickler," sighed Airy Fairy.

Scary Fairy gave Airy Fairy a sly poke with her wand. "Dumb fairy," she smirked.

Airy Fairy poked her right back.

"And stop poking Scary Fairy with your
wand, or you'll have extra homework to do,
even if it IS the last day of term," warned
Miss Stickler.

"Yes, Miss Stickler," sighed Airy Fairy again.
It was always the same. Scary Fairy, who
was Miss Stickler's niece, always picked on
her. Airy Fairy didn't know why.

"Never mind, Airy Fairy," whispered Buttercup
and Tingle, when Airy Fairy had picked up her
pens and pencils and sat down again. "We'll
give you a hand to clear out your desk."

In no time at all, they helped Airy Fairy throw out all the broken pencils, all the scrunched-up paper, and all the half-chewed candies, not forgetting the empty yogurt container.

"There," they beamed. "Now you're ready for summer vacation."

"Thank you," said Airy Fairy, and cupped her chin in her hands and smiled. She really

loved Fairy Gropplethorpe's Academy for Good Fairies, despite Scary Fairy. To passersby, the school just looked like an abandoned tree house, high up in an old oak, but inside it was home to ten little orphaned fairies. Airy Fairy smiled again. She especially loved Fairy Gropplethorpe's Academy in the summertime when vacation began. That meant no hard math problems, no difficult spelling, and no tricky flying-backward lessons. She had enough trouble flying forward. Now it was six long weeks of doing nothing but play.

"Hooray for summer vacation," she cried, as the classroom door opened and Fairy Gropplethorpe came in, accompanied by Rainbow and Macduff.

"I'm glad to see you all looking so happy, Fairies," smiled Fairy Gropplethorpe. "And since you have worked so hard this term, I have a surprise for you. You are all going on a special vacation. There will be no hard math problems and no difficult spelling to do, so you can leave your fairy wands behind."

"Ooh, are we going to the beach again?" asked Airy Fairy. "I just love the beach. I love splashing around in the rock pools. I love making sand castles. Can we have a sand castle competition like we did last year? I'm going to try to make one with turrets and a moat and..."

"Airy Fairy, do be quiet and listen to Fairy Gropplethorpe."

"Yes, Miss Stickler. Sorry, Miss Stickler. Sorry, Fairy Gropplethorpe."

Fairy Gropplethorpe smiled again. "I know you're all excited about vacation, but I'm afraid I won't be able to take you to the beach this year. I have just discovered a hole in the school roof and must stay here until the builders arrive to fix it. But Miss Stickler has kindly volunteered to take you all on a trip, though I don't think it's to the beach."

"Oh." Airy Fairy's face fell.

"No," said Miss Stickler. "This year we're not going to the beach to get ourselves covered in gritty brown sand. This year we're going to do something much more educational. This year we're going camping."

"Camping?" Airy Fairy's face fell even further. "Oh, I don't think I'll like that. There are bound to be creepy, crawly things, and busy, buzzy things, and big, ENORMOUS spiders…"

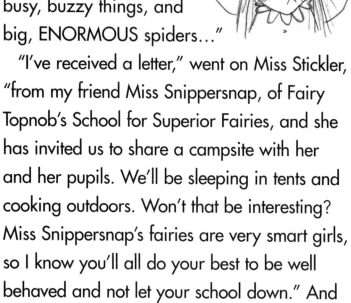

"I've received a letter," went on Miss Stickler, "from my friend Miss Snippersnap, of Fairy Topnob's School for Superior Fairies, and she has invited us to share a campsite with her and her pupils. We'll be sleeping in tents and cooking outdoors. Won't that be interesting? Miss Snippersnap's fairies are very smart girls, so I know you'll all do your best to be well behaved and not let your school down." And she looked meaningfully at Airy Fairy.

Airy Fairy didn't notice. She was too busy worrying about the camping and the spiders. There was a lot that could go wrong for a fairy in a field.

"It sounds wonderful," said Fairy Gropplethorpe, "and I shall join you as soon as I can. Meanwhile, off you go and have fun."

And Fairy Gropplethorpe bustled away with Rainbow and Macduff to worry about the school roof.

"Now, Fairies," said Miss Stickler. "Here is a list of what you need to take for the camping trip, so hurry along to your bedrooms and pack your knapsacks. We're leaving this afternoon."

"Oh dear," said Airy Fairy, picking up her copy of the list. "I don't think I want to sleep on a door or cook a tent. I'm sure to get it all wrong. I'm sure this vacation will be a disaster."

"No, it won't," soothed Buttercup and Tingle. "Stop worrying, Airy Fairy. You'll be fine."

"No, you won't," muttered Scary Fairy slyly. "I'm sneaking my wand with me, and I'll see that you're not."

Chapter Two

Airy Fairy flew upstairs to her bedroom to look for her little knapsack.

"I think that might be one of its red straps hanging down from my big cabinet," she said, and gave the strap a tug. WHUMPH. Down came the knapsack on top of her, along with a pail and shovel, a pair of flippers and some goggles, and some pink and white striped sunglasses.

"Oh," she gasped, picking herself up from the floor. "I wondered where all those things had gone." And she looked at the list Miss Stickler had given her. "But I'm not supposed to pack any of them for this vacation." Instead she had to pack her parka and rubber boots, her knit hat and scarf, and a big, warm sweater.

"Those don't sound very much like vacation things," said Airy Fairy. "Perhaps Miss Stickler's forgotten to mention a bathing suit and some shorts. I'd better put mine in anyway. And my flippers and goggles. You can't go swimming without flippers and goggles. And what about my snorkel? I'd better put that in, too."

Then she sat back and looked at the list again. "It doesn't say anything about puzzles either," she muttered. "I always like to do a puzzle on vacation." And she rummaged through the bottom of her closet, found one of her favorites, and tossed that in her knapsack, too.

"Oh, and I can't forget pocket Ted. He likes to go on vacation, too." And she tied a scarf around Ted's neck and put him in the pocket of her pink fairy jeans. She left his head sticking out.

"So you can see where we're going, Ted," she explained.

Then she tried to close her knapsack. It wasn't easy. It was full of lumps and bumps. She had to jump on them to squash them down.

Airy Fairy's face was as pink as her jeans by the time she got the knapsack closed. Then she looked around at the pail and shovel and pink and white striped sunglasses, still lying on her bedroom floor.

"I might need these, too," she said. And she found some string and tied the pail and shovel onto the outside of the knapsack, and put on her sunglasses.

"OK, Ted. Here we go."

But they didn't. Airy Fairy puffed and panted, and panted and puffed, but she couldn't even lift the knapsack, never mind put it on her back.

"Oh, boy," she said. "This is far too heavy for me. I'm going to have to try a spell to get it down into the hall."

Ted closed his eyes and crossed his paws.

Airy Fairy took off her sunglasses, found her wand, and gave it a wave.

"ALL FOR ONE
AND ONE FOR ALL
PLEASE TAKE THIS KNAPSACK
TO THE HALL!"

WHOOSH! The knapsack sailed out through the bedroom door, down the stairs, and straight into Miss Stickler, knocking her over.

"Oh, my! Oh, sorry, Miss Stickler," said Airy Fairy, dropping her wand and flying downstairs to help her. "I had just finished packing, but the knapsack was very heavy and I couldn't lift it, and I did a spell, but I don't think it could have been the right one, and I must have gotten it mixed up and..."

Airy Fairy patted Miss Stickler's head. "Is your head very sore? Can I get you a bandage? Do you put bandages on bumps? Or, I could get you a wet washcloth, or I could…"

"You will do nothing, Airy Fairy," cried Miss Stickler, staggering to her feet. "Nothing at all, except stand right here. Do not move from this spot. We haven't even left to go on our trip yet, and already you're in trouble. I hope you are not going to let the Academy down when we meet up with Miss Snippersnap's fairies."

"Yes, Miss Stickler. I mean no, Miss Stickler. I mean sorry, Miss Stickler. I just don't know what happened to that spell. I was sure I got it right..."

"You did, until I mixed it up," giggled Scary Fairy to herself as she flew downstairs with her little knapsack. "And there are plenty more mix-ups where that came from, Airy Fairy. I don't know why everyone likes you so much. You're such a fool. You're going to be an absolute disaster on this vacation. I've packed my wand to make sure of that."

Chapter Three

Miss Stickler had arranged for a toy Fairy Tour bus to take the fairies to the campsite, and, when it arrived at the foot of the oak tree, all the fairies flew down and put their knapsacks into the trunk. All except Airy Fairy.

"Your knapsack is far too heavy, Airy
Fairy," frowned Miss Stickler. "But there is no
time to unpack it now, or we will be late
arriving at the campsite." And she waved
her wand and magicked Airy Fairy's
knapsack out of the school and down to the
bus below.

Airy Fairy flew down after it. But she still
couldn't lift it into the trunk.

"Here, I'll give you a hand, little Fairy,"
said Elvis Elf, the bus driver. "Watcha got in
here, anyway? The kitchen sink?" he puffed
as he heaved it into the trunk.

"Oh, no, that wasn't on the list," said Airy Fairy, shaking her head.

Elvis Elf chuckled and went over to speak to Miss Stickler, so he didn't see Airy Fairy climb in after her knapsack to make sure her pail and shovel were still securely tied on.

She'd just finished checking when ... WHAM, the trunk lid shut and Airy Fairy was left in the dark.

"Oh, no," she cried. "Help! Help!" But no one could hear her above the noise of the bus starting up. "Help," she yelled again as she felt the bus vibrate along the ground and start to lift off into the air. "Help," she yelled again as the front of the bus tilted upward and she slid and banged her head on the inside of the trunk.

And she might have spent the whole ride to the campsite in the trunk of the bus, if Buttercup and Tingle hadn't noticed she was missing and alerted Miss Stickler.

Suddenly Airy Fairy felt her ears pop as the bus descended quickly, bounced along the ground again and came to a stop back at the foot of the oak tree. She yelled and thumped her shovel on the inside of the trunk.

"That can only be Airy Fairy," sighed Miss Stickler.

Elvis Elf and Miss Stickler got out of the bus and opened up the trunk. They found Airy Fairy still yelling, "Help, get me out of here," and banging on the side of the bus with her shovel.

"AIRY FAIRY," it was Miss Stickler's turn to yell. "Get on the bus this minute and DO not move a muscle until we get to the campsite. In fact, DO nothing. SAY nothing. DO you understand?"

Airy Fairy looked at her with big eyes and said nothing.

"DO YOU UNDERSTAND?" Miss Stickler yelled even louder.

Airy Fairy looked at her with even bigger eyes and still said nothing.

"CAN YOU HEAR ME?" yelled Miss Stickler.

"I should think half the country can hear you," muttered Elvis Elf. "Glad I'm not still at school."

This time Airy Fairy nodded her head slightly and hurried on to the bus. *I wish teachers wouldn't tell you to say nothing, then ask you questions, she thought. It makes life very difficult.*

The Fairy Tour bus took off again and, after passing over lots of patchwork fields and little villages, landed at the campsite. It was in a muddy field with enormous cows.

"Ah, Miss Stickler," said Miss Snippersnap, hurrying forward to meet them. "You and your fairies are here at last. I was beginning to think you'd gotten lost. That's your accommodation over there." And she pointed to a row of tents.

"Oh, no," said Airy Fairy, who had decided it was safe to speak by now. "I hope these cows don't notice our tents. I hope they don't think I'm lunch."

"Of course they won't," said Buttercup and Tingle. "Cows only eat grass, and anyway we're so small they won't even see us."

"That's what you think," muttered Scary Fairy. "I'm sure I can have some fun with them."

Miss Stickler showed the fairies to their tents. "Now, unpack your things and assemble at my tent in fifteen minutes when you hear me peep my silver whistle," she said.

Airy Fairy's tent was right beside Miss Stickler's. "I've put you where I can keep an eye on you, Airy Fairy," she said. "I don't want you causing any more trouble."

"Yes, Miss Stickler. I mean no, Miss Stickler," muttered Airy Fairy, and ducked into her tent.

It was tiny inside. Hardly enough room for
Airy Fairy, never mind her bulging knapsack.
"What's this?" she said, spotting a rolled-up
bundle at the far end. "It must be my
sleeping bag. I've never slept in one of these
before. I'd better unroll it and try it out while
it's still daytime. It might be a bit tricky
tonight by flashlight."

Airy Fairy unrolled the sleeping bag,
climbed inside, and zipped herself up.

"Hmm," she said, rolling around on the ground, trying to get comfortable. "I think I'd rather have my little fairy bed at school." She rolled around a little more and knocked over her knapsack. It knocked over the tent pole and the tent fell down on top of her.

"Oh, no," muttered Airy Fairy. "It's all dark. I must fix this tent before Miss Stickler notices. I'm in enough trouble already." And she propped the tent pole back up as best she could. "Now, I'll just get myself out of this sleeping bag."

But she couldn't. The zipper was caught in her fairy jeans, and, try as she might, she couldn't set herself free. She wriggled around for ages, then ... PEEP PEEP...

"Oh, no," she cried. "That's Miss Stickler's whistle. I have to assemble outside her tent, and I can't get out of this sleeping bag. What am I going to do?" She wriggled around some more, but it was no use. "I'll just have to go like this," she sighed.

"AIRY FAIRY," yelled Miss Stickler, as Airy Fairy came hopping toward her wearing her sleeping bag.

"I'm sorry, Miss Stickler," panted Airy
Fairy. "I was just trying out my sleeping bag
before it got dark, and the zipper got stuck.
The tent fell down on top of me, too."

The other fairies started giggling. They just
loved Airy Fairy. She always made them
laugh. They all went to help her out of the
sleeping bag.

All except Scary Fairy. She wasn't laughing and she didn't go to help. "I just don't understand it. Why does everyone like her so much?" she muttered. "She always gets things wrong."

Miss Stickler wasn't laughing either. Miss Snippersnap had noticed the commotion and had come to investigate.

"Not a very good start to your camping vacation, Miss Stickler," she sniffed. "None of MY fairies would be silly enough to get stuck in a sleeping bag."

Miss Stickler's face was grim as Miss Snippersnap strode off. The last thing she wanted was for her fairies to look bad. "Now Airy Fairy is really in trouble," she muttered.

Scary Fairy was delighted and patted the fairy wand in her pocket. *And I'm sure I can get her into lots more,* she thought.

Chapter Four

But Airy Fairy was determined to try to stay out of trouble, so when Miss Stickler announced their camp duties, she listened very carefully.

"Silvie and Skelf are in charge of collecting water from the farm over yonder," said Miss Stickler, pointing to a long, gray structure, which to humans just looked like an upturned sink.

"Buttercup and Tingle and Cherri and Honeysuckle will go with them and carefully collect an egg for our dinner. Twink and Plink will go and organize games with Miss Snippersnap and her fairies. Scary Fairy, since she is the most responsible fairy –" Miss Stickler stopped reading from her list, and beamed at her niece – "will be in charge of our campfire. And Airy Fairy, since she is the most irresponsible fairy, will collect the wood from the forest."

And Miss Stickler turned and frowned at Airy Fairy. "Even you should be able to do that without getting into trouble," she said.

Airy Fairy nodded and looked over at the forest. It was on the edge of the field behind their tents.

"I'll go right away," she said, anxious to please, and flew off. In two minutes she was there. "This forest is really nice," she said, as she flitted through the trees. "I wonder if I'll see any red squirrels." And she looked up through the branches. Then she remembered she was supposed to be looking for firewood and looked down at the ground. BOINK. She crashed into a large pine tree and slid down the trunk.

"Oh, dear," she sighed, rubbing her bumps and bruises. "Always remember to look where you're going, Airy Fairy," and she got up, straightened her wings, and began to look for firewood. There was plenty of dry kindling littering the forest floor and she soon had a large bundle.

"Miss Stickler is bound to be pleased with this," she said, beaming, and started to fly out of the forest. But she had gathered so much kindling that pieces kept falling to the ground.

"Maybe I better just walk back," she muttered, "or I'll have no wood left."

But there was a problem. The cows had moved and were in between her and the campsite.

Airy Fairy gulped and walked toward them. "Nice cows, good cows, never mind about a fairy and her wood, cows," she whispered.

"Mooooo," went the cows loudly.

Airy Fairy nearly jumped out of her boots and dropped all her wood.

She quickly picked it up again, keeping an anxious eye on the cows. "I'll just try and go around the edge of them," she muttered.

As quietly as she could, she tiptoed around the outside of the herd muttering to herself, "Cows are good, cows are nice, cows won't look at a fairy twice."

But Scary Fairy, waiting impatiently for the wood to arrive for the campfire, spotted Airy Fairy tiptoeing away from the cows.

"Aha." She smiled slyly. "Now for some fun." And, when no one was looking, she took out her wand and gave it a little wave.

Suddenly, the cows lifted their heads and started to chase Airy Fairy.

"Help," cried Airy Fairy and flapped her battered wings and began to fly. Bit by bit, the wood for the campfire slipped from her grasp and bopped the cows on their noses.

This annoyed them even more and they chased Airy Fairy right back to the campsite, trampling all the tents as they passed.

Then they stopped as suddenly as they'd begun, looked confused, and wandered back the way they came.

"Now how on earth did that happen?" Airy Fairy wondered as she bumped down to the ground, exhausted.

Miss Stickler was almost speechless. "Airy Fairy, how could..."

"I couldn't help it, Miss Stickler," gasped Airy Fairy. "I had the firewood, and I was tiptoeing around the cows, but they started chasing me, and I lost it all." And she looked around at all the trampled tents. "Oh, dear," she said. "Sorry, Miss Stickler."

"Sorry isn't good enough, Airy Fairy." Miss Stickler had recovered her power of speech. "Of course you could help it. Cows don't just start chasing fairies. As usual, this is all your fault."

Airy Fairy traced a circle on the grass with the toe of her boot. "Sorry, Miss Stickler."

But Miss Stickler wasn't finished yet. "Now Twink and Plink have arranged a baseball game with Miss Snippersnap's fairies, but you will stay here and put up all the tents instead. Then you will go back and collect the wood you dropped WITHOUT disturbing the cows. Do you understand?"

"Yes, Miss Stickler," said Airy Fairy miserably. She would have liked to play baseball. That sounded like fun.

Scary Fairy grinned victoriously.

Buttercup and Tingle offered to stay behind to help Airy Fairy with the tents, but Miss Stickler would not hear of it.

"Airy Fairy must learn to stay out of trouble," she said. And everyone went off leaving Airy Fairy alone.

Airy Fairy gave the biggest sigh in the universe and started sorting out the tents. Hammering in lots of tent pegs is hard work for one little fairy. When she had finished, she very cautiously flew back into the forest to collect the firewood. This time the cows didn't even look at her. They just went on contentedly eating the grass.

"Hmm, I wonder if Scary Fairy was up to her tricks that last time," said Airy Fairy. But by now, she was too tired to care.

Buttercup and Tingle looked into her tent when they came back from their baseball game. "Come and sit around the campfire while we boil the egg for dinner," they started to say. But Airy Fairy and pocket Ted were already tucked up in their little sleeping bag fast asleep.

Chapter Five

The next morning, all the fairies were up bright and early, especially Airy Fairy.

"I'm starving," she said to Buttercup and Tingle. "I missed my bit of the boiled egg for dinner last night."

Miss Stickler, wearing shorts and a wool sweater, was making oatmeal in a big, black pot over the campfire.

"Breakfast will be ready soon, Fairies," she said, beaming. "Just go down to the stream to wash your hands and faces."

The fairies collected their small overnight bags and towels and headed for the stream that bordered the field. When they arrived, Miss Snippersnap's fairies were already there.

"Where's the fairy who stampeded the cows?" they asked.

"Here she is," said Scary Fairy, pushing Airy Fairy to the front. "But look out for her, she's a fool."

"She must be," laughed Miss Snippersnap's fairies. "No one from Fairy Topnob's School for Superior Fairies would ever do anything so dumb." And they all turned and ignored Airy Fairy. They lined up neatly at the edge of the stream, and dipped their washcloths delicately into the water.

Airy Fairy sighed and looked in her overnight bag. She had forgotten her washcloth.

Oh well, she thought. *I'll just have to splash water on my face instead.* And she bent down toward the stream. That's when she noticed the fish darting in and out among the pebbles on the stream bed.

"Oh," she breathed, "aren't they lovely. Just like flashing silver." And she leaned forward to get a closer look.

Scary Fairy saw her chance. When no one was watching she waved her little wand. Suddenly, there was a huge gust of wind that WHOOSHED Airy Fairy sideways.

"Help!" gasped Airy Fairy, her legs and arms going everywhere.

"Help!" gasped the Superior Fairies, as Airy Fairy banged into them and knocked them all over like a row of dominoes, and they toppled into the water.

"Ooh, aah, help!" they gasped, as they struggled, dripping from the stream.

"You did that on purpose, you dumb, foolish fairy." They surrounded Airy Fairy. "Just wait until Miss Snippersnap hears about this."

"Oh, no," gasped Airy Fairy. "I didn't … I don't know … I mean … what will Miss Stickler say now!"

Miss Stickler said plenty. She had been happily stirring her oatmeal when Miss Snippersnap arrived to tell her all about it. At great length.

"Just keep that silly fairy away from my girls," Miss Snippersnap warned Miss Stickler. "She is obviously a menace. I would never have invited you here if I'd known there would be so much trouble."

Miss Stickler wasn't pleased, and she certainly didn't believe Airy Fairy's story about a big wind coming and whooshing her sideways. "But the big wind didn't blow over anyone else, did it, Airy Fairy?" she stormed. "Just you, oddly enough."

"But Airy Fairy didn't mean it, Miss Stickler." Buttercup and Tingle tried to stand up for her. "It all just sort of happened. Like perhaps someone had brought their wand…"

Airy Fairy nodded. She had a good idea who that someone might be, but it wasn't nice to tell tales, and Miss Stickler would never believe her anyway.

But Miss Stickler wasn't listening. "I'm going to take the other fairies to collect milk from the farm, but you will remain here, Airy Fairy.

Scary Fairy will set the breakfast table and keep an eye on you. Take this wooden spoon and stir the oatmeal. Even you should be able to do that without getting into any more trouble."

"Yes, Miss Stickler," sighed Airy Fairy, and she took the wooden spoon. She looked into the big, black pot. The oatmeal was making soft, little plopping noises. Airy Fairy stirred the oatmeal gently and it heaved its way slowly around the pot.

"I don't really like being left alone with Scary Fairy when she's up to her tricks. She might magic up enormous spiders," she said, and looked around anxiously. "And I don't know if I really like oatmeal, but I'm so hungry I could eat three whole bowls." And she gave it another gentle stir.

When the others were out of sight and Airy Fairy was busy stirring, Scary Fairy peered out of her tent and saw another chance to get Airy Fairy into trouble. She smiled slyly and waved her little magic wand.

WHEEE. The oatmeal sped up and started whizzing around in the pot.

"Help, what's happening?" cried Airy Fairy, trying to keep up with the oatmeal with her wooden spoon. "Stop, oatmeal. Stop!"

But it didn't stop. Instead, it whizzed around faster and faster and started making angry slurping noises.

"Stop, please. Stop!" yelled Airy Fairy. But the oatmeal began erupting like a little volcano, splashing out of the pot and on to the grass.

"Stop, oatmeal. Stop!" yelled Airy Fairy, her little arm whizzing around, and nearly dropping off with the effort of trying to control it.

But the oatmeal wouldn't stop. It threw out more and more splashes until the pot was completely empty. The gloopy oatmeal was all over the ground, all over the campfire, which it had put out, and all over Airy Fairy.

Miss Stickler arrived back with the other fairies just in time to see Airy Fairy trying to scoop some of the grassy oatmeal back into the pot.

"I'm so sorry, Aunt Stickler," Scary Fairy said at once. "I don't know how she managed it. I just turned my back for a moment to go into the storage tent to collect the bowls and spoons for the oatmeal, and look what happened."

"Don't worry, Scary Fairy," said Miss Stickler. "It's not your fault. It's not your fault that we shall have nothing but cold milk and dry biscuits for breakfast, instead of delicious, creamy oatmeal. As usual, this is all your fault, Airy Fairy. You will take that oatmeal pot down to the stream and give it a good cleaning."

Buttercup and Tingle offered to go and help Airy Fairy, but Miss Stickler wouldn't let them.

"Airy Fairy must be punished for her terrible behavior. She never wanted to come on this trip, and she's just trying to ruin it for everyone else. I will not have that."

And Airy Fairy had to lug the big pot down to the stream and give it a good cleaning.

But, as soon as they could, Buttercup and Tingle slipped away and helped Airy Fairy bring the clean pot back.

"Look," they whispered. "We saved you some biscuits. You must be starving."

"I am," said Airy Fairy, and had a quick bite. "But I'm not trying to spoil the vacation for everyone else. Really, I'm not."

"We know that," said Buttercup and Tingle. "It's Scary Fairy up to her dirty tricks again. But we'll help you keep an eye on her, and so will the other fairies."

"Thank you. But Scary Fairy's just too clever to get caught," sighed Airy Fairy. "This is such a rotten vacation, I almost wish I was back in school doing hard math problems and difficult spelling. Surely things can't get any worse."

But they did.

Chapter Six

Later that day, it started to rain. Not a light, refreshing rain, but a heavy downpour that went on and on. Airy Fairy sat in her little tent with Ted. He was warm and dry in her pocket, but she was cold and wet as water dripped from the roof of her tent down the neck of her parka, and seeped up from the ground through a hole in the sole of her boot.

But Miss Stickler didn't mind the rain. PEEP
PEEP went her silver whistle.

"Come along, Fairies," she cried, "a little
rain never hurt anyone. Miss Snippersnap's
fairies are here to join us on a nature hunt."

"I'd like to hunt out somewhere dry,"
muttered Airy Fairy, as she squelched out of
her tent and into a big puddle. Her right
boot filled up with water and she had to take
it off and empty it out.

"Hurry along, Airy Fairy," said Miss
Stickler.

Airy Fairy tried to hurry along, but she couldn't get her foot all the way back into the damp boot. She hobbled along with the boot half on, half off, skidded on the muddy grass, and fell into another big puddle.

"What a messy fairy," sniffed Miss Snippersnap's girls. "Don't come anywhere near us."

"She just slipped, that's all," said Buttercup and Tingle.

"It could happen to anyone in this weather," said Cherri and Honeysuckle.

"It wouldn't happen to me," smirked Scary Fairy.

But the rest of Fairy Gropplethorpe's fairies just glared at her and gathered around Airy Fairy and helped her up.

"Now here is a list of three things you have to hunt for," said Miss Stickler. "The first fairy to return with all three items will win a large bag of lollipops."

"Oh, is that all," sniffed Miss Snippersnap's fairies. "We thought it would at least be a box of super fancy chocolates."

"I'm sure to win the prize anyway," said Scary Fairy, "since I'm the cleverest fairy." And she set off immediately with her list.

Airy Fairy looked at hers. She had to find a four-leaf clover, a seed from a dandelion stem, and a petal from a buttercup.

"Come on, everyone," said Twink and Plink. "Scary Fairy's got a head start. Let's catch up to her."

All the fairies found a buttercup petal right away. The field was full of buttercups. Airy

Fairy rolled hers up and put it into the pocket of her parka. Then she started looking for a dandelion seed.

"Oh, we've found ours already. This is too easy." Miss Snippersnap's fairies gave a sniff. Big mistake. They sniffed their dandelion seeds right up their snooty noses.

"Ooh," they cried. "How terrible." And they got out their dainty handkerchiefs and began to blow and blow.

Airy Fairy grinned, found her dandelion seed, and tucked it carefully into the pocket of her parka.

"Just the four-leaf clover to find now," she said. "Miss Stickler will be pleased if one of our fairies wins the prize."

But it was very hard to find a four-leaf clover, especially in the rain. All the fairies were still searching, including Scary Fairy.

"I want that prize. I must be the one to find it," she muttered.

But she wasn't.

Airy Fairy stopped in her search to empty out her boot again, and there on the grass, right where she was hopping around on one foot, was a four-leaf clover.

"I found it. I found it," she yelled, slipping and sliding on the wet grass as she held it up above her head. "I found a four-leaf clover."

"Oh no, you haven't," muttered Scary Fairy, and took out her wand to whisk it away.

But Fairy Gropplethorpe's other fairies had been keeping an eye on Scary Fairy.

"Oh no, you don't," they said, and whisked Scary Fairy's wand away from her and dropped it in the stream.

Scary Fairy had no choice but to wade in after it. "Aa, aah, a-a-achoo! I'll get you for this," she sneezed, as she flapped around in the muddy water.

But the fairies ignored her. They just hurried back with Airy Fairy to collect the prize.

Miss Stickler was pleased that one of her fairies had won. "I just didn't think it would be you, Airy Fairy," she said. "Well done."

"We didn't want the silly lollipops anyway," sniffed Miss Snippersnap's fairies and delicately stomped off.

"Fine," grinned Airy Fairy. "That means more for us," and she shared the lollipops among her friends.

"I don't want one ob dem eider," muttered Scary Fairy, as she slunk back into her tent to change into dry clothes.

The fairies looked at each other and giggled. They were just enjoying their lollipops when there was an unexpected arrival.

"Look," cried Airy Fairy, pointing to the sky. "It's Elvis Elf's Fairy Tour bus."

Everyone watched as the Fairy Tour bus

zoomed down from the sky, bounced through
the muddy field, and came to a stop beside the
fairies.

Out hopped Rainbow and Macduff, followed
by Fairy Gropplethorpe.

"Good news, Fairies," she beamed. "The
school roof wasn't as bad as I thought and
now I can start my summer vacation, too. But
I've just seen the weather forecast. It's going to
stay very wet around here, but it's nice and
sunny at the beach. So I've come to take you
all there instead."

"Hurray," cried all the fairies, except Scary Fairy. She could only croak.

Miss Stickler shook her head. "I'm afraid this wet weather has been bad for poor Scary Fairy. She can't possibly come with you. I'll take her back to school, and put her to bed instead."

"Oh, what a shame," said the other fairies, and tried not to laugh.

The fairies climbed onto the bus and Elvis Elf helped Airy Fairy put her knapsack into the trunk. He made sure she was safe inside the bus this time.

Then Fairy Gropplethorpe said, "OK, Mr. Elf. Take Miss Stickler and Scary Fairy back to school, then take the rest of us to the beach."

"Right away, Fairy Gropplethorpe," grinned Elvis Elf and switched on his engine.

Airy Fairy sat back in her seat and smiled happily. "I knew I was right to pack my pail and shovel," she said to Tingle and Buttercup. "I just love the beach."

Meet Airy Fairy.

Her wand is bent, her wings
are covered in bandages,
and her spells are always a muddle!
But she's the cutest fairy around!

Look for the other books
in this series...

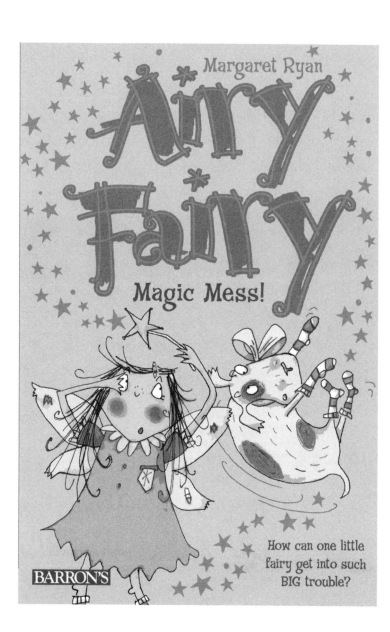

Margaret Ryan

Airy Fairy

Magic Mess!

How can one little
fairy get into such
BIG trouble?

BARRON'S

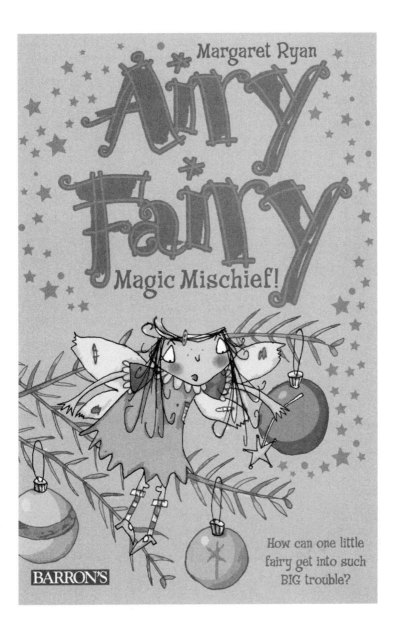

Margaret Ryan

Airy Fairy

Magic Mischief!

BARRON'S

How can one little
fairy get into such
BIG trouble?